Ghost Horse

The horse turned its head towards her. Its eyes were gentle and intelligent. It seemed to know she felt sorry for it.

Shona cautiously drew a little nearer. Though she felt sorry for the horse and fascinated by it, she was still afraid of it.

The beautiful creature whinnied softly. "Help me," its soft brown eyes seemed to say. "Please help me," they pleaded.

If you enjoy *Ghost Horse*, dare you try *Ghost Dog*, also by Eleanor Allen?

And if you're *really* brave, there are all these other Young Hippo Spookies to enjoy!

Mystery Valentine
Carol Barton

The Screaming Demon Ghostie
Jean Chapman

The Ghost of Able Mabel
Penny Dolan

The Ghost Hunter
Ivan Jones

The Green Hand
Tessa Krailing

Smoke Cat
Linda Newbery

Bumps in the Night
Frank Rodgers

Spooky Movie
Claire Ronan

The Kings' Castle
Ann Ruffell

Scarem's House
Malcolm Yorke

ELEANOR ALLEN

Ghost Horse

Inside illustrations by Peter Kavanagh

Hippo

For Barbara and Peter

Scholastic Children's Books,
Commonwealth House, 1-19 New Oxford Street,
London WC1A 1NU, UK
a division of Scholastic Ltd
London ~ New York ~ Toronto ~ Sydney ~ Auckland

Published in the UK by Scholastic Ltd, 1998

Text copyright © Eleanor Allen, 1998
Inside illustrations copyright © Peter Kavanagh, 1998
Cover illustration copyright © Anne Sharp, 1998

ISBN 0 590 19709 6

Printed by Cox & Wyman Ltd, Reading, Berks.

4 6 8 10 9 7 5 3

Chapter 1

"Would you like to go riding in the summer holidays?" asked Shona's mum. "I've booked a cottage on a beautiful moor called Exmoor. It's the perfect place for riding."

"No," said Shona glumly. "You know I hate horses."

"Still?" sighed her mum.

"Yes," said Shona. "And I always shall."

When the time for their holiday came round, Shona and her mum and dad drove across the wide, open spaces of Exmoor, until they reached a large and pretty village near the sea. Their car drew up outside a white-painted cottage with black window frames and tiny panes of old glass. Hanging low over the bedroom windows was a thick, thatched roof.

Shona liked the look of their holiday cottage, but her mum had doubts.

"It's built straight on to the main street," she frowned. "I hope it won't be noisy."

"The brochure said it used to be an old coaching inn. So it would be on the main street, wouldn't it?" Dad pointed out.

"Why are there three stone steps standing in the road and going nowhere?" asked Shona.

"That's an old mounting block," said Mum. "Left over from when this was an inn. Travellers stood on top to mount their horses."

"Wonder what else is left over from the old inn days?" grinned Dad. "I could fancy a pint of beer."

Inside, there were a few low oak beams and some rather uneven floors, to remind them that this was once the Old Bull Inn. But no roaring log fires, four-poster beds and rush-strewn floors. Just a gas fire, a fitted carpet and a modern kitchen. It was clean and comfortable, but Shona felt disappointed by the inside.

Dad said some of the old stabling was still there, round the back. He had put the car in it because it was now a garage.

"Thinking of stabling," said Shona's mum, "I noticed several farms near here have ponies and horses for hire. Wouldn't it be wonderful to ride over the moor tomorrow? Have you changed your mind about riding, Shona?"

"No," said Shona firmly. "I haven't. And I never shall. I've told you already – I *hate* horses. I'll *walk* over the moor."

Chapter 2

Once upon a time, Shona had loved horses. More than that – she had been mad about them. She'd had a few riding lessons and had been getting on just fine.

Then a friend from school called Sarah had got a pony of her own. She had invited Shona over to ride him.

Sarah's pony was a cocky little chap

called Taffy and he lived in a field behind Sarah's house. Everybody said Taffy was as good as gold. Safe as houses. And so he was. Apart from one very big flaw. And in all the excitement over showing him off, nobody remembered to warn Shona before she mounted him.

Flop, flap, flop, went Shona's waterproof jacket as the wind caught it.

Taffy pricked up his ears. What strange noise was that, on his back? He didn't like it.

Taffy knew he more than didn't like it – he was scared of it. More than scared – terrified! He wanted to get away from it. He panicked. He kicked up his heels and bolted away down the field. Shocked out of her wits, Shona screamed and clung on tight.

Sarah, her big brother Tom and her mum were in the field. But there was nothing they could do.

For a second or two, Shona was so busy screaming and trying not to fall off, she didn't notice where they were heading –

straight for a prickly hawthorn hedge.
When she did see it, she panicked too!
She was about to fling herself off. But at
that moment, Taffy thought of a different
way to rid himself of the scary noise.

He bucked and shot Shona off.

The ground seemed to rise up and hit Shona like a great iron fist. She lay bruised and shaken and very, very shocked. As she gazed up at the high, prickly hawthorn hedge, she shuddered. She had almost landed in that!

Sarah, with her brother and mum, ran to pick her up and check for broken bones. They were relieved she seemed okay. They caught Taffy and calmed him down, then explained to her what had happened.

"You should take your jacket off and get back up," they urged. "You have to get your confidence back. Up you get."

White-faced and tense, Shona refused.
She didn't want to get back up – not on
Taffy, not on any horse. Ever again.

Horses weren't fun to Shona any
more. They did strange things she
couldn't control. Horses were dangerous,
unpredictable creatures – creatures to
fear.

Chapter 3

A wind from the sea was sweeping over the moor that afternoon. It was a feather-ruffling, boat-buffeting wind with an icy sharp edge to it, like the cut of waves. It lifted Shona's hair and plucked at her skirt as she ran across the cobbled yard behind the Old Bull Inn towards the garage. She had left her book in the car.

The garage was a sheltered spot. It smelled faintly of petrol and cooling-down metal. Shona took her mum's keys from her pocket and unlocked the car. She took her book from the back seat and locked up again carefully.

The warmth of the garage seemed welcoming. Shona looked around. It was built of old blocks of orangey-pink and grey-green stone. Set high up was a round-shaped window, edged with brick. Sunshine was streaming through the window, bathing the far end of the building in a golden light. That end was piled with junk – broken furniture, rusting tools and empty paint tins. And there was an old wooden partition of some sort too. Shona felt curious to know what was behind it.

It was an empty stall. The only one still

left from the days when this had been stabling for the busy coaching inn.

Shona sniffed and her face turned pale.

Horse!

Shona sniffed again. The smell was stronger now, and getting stronger all the time. Warm and strong, it overpowered the smell of car.

The rays of sun dazzled her eyes.

Shona put up a hand to shade them. She blinked. And when she looked again into the empty stall, it wasn't empty any more.

A horse was standing there.

Shona screamed. It was a piercing, blood-curdling scream inside her. But what came out was shrivelled and shrunken. More like a gasp.

Shona's hand gripped the side of the stall. Her brain told her to run away, but her body wouldn't move.

It was no more than a shadow horse at first. But before her eyes, it began to flesh out, into a solid horse. Not a horse for pulling coaches. Not an ordinary horse – a magnificent horse.

It was a stallion, the colour of polished steel, with a mane and tail like pure white, silken thread. A horse so beautiful, it took Shona's breath away.

Though she still trembled from head to toe, a feeling of delight and wonderment crept over her. She stared at the horse as if bound by a spell.

The horse stirred; it stamped a hoof and flicked its ears. It knew that she was there.

Then Shona gasped in pity and surprise. For on the horse's legs she saw some nasty cuts. Another wound was bleeding on its flank and its neck had been grazed by a rope.

"What happened to you?" she whispered.

The horse turned its head towards her. Its eyes were gentle and intelligent. It seemed to know she felt sorry for it.

Shona cautiously drew a little nearer. Though she felt sorry for the horse and fascinated by it, she was still afraid of it.

The beautiful creature whinnied softly. "Help me," its soft brown eyes seemed to say. "Please help me," they pleaded.

Shona's knees felt trembly. She shook her head unhappily. "Why are you asking me? I'm scared of horses. I can't help you."

"I know you're afraid," the horse's eyes seemed to say. "But you must overcome your fear. Then you can help me."

"How can I help you?" Shona asked nervously.

"Come nearer, don't be scared. Come closer," urged the horse. "Touch me, touch me…"

Shona drew a little nearer. She put out a trembling hand. It hovered fearfully over the horse's flank. She felt his warmth. She almost touched...

"Shona! Shona! We're going out to eat!"

Her mother's voice rang out across the yard. A shrill voice from the human world. And the warm horse flesh began to fade away.

"Oh, don't go," Shona whispered. "Please don't go...!"

But the horse had already gone. Her mum had scared it away.

Shona didn't tell Mum about the horse. She knew it was a secret between the two of them.

She wondered how the poor, beautiful creature had been injured. And if she would ever see it again.

And why it was a ghost horse, needing her help.

THE HIGHWAYMAN

Chapter 4

That evening, Shona and her mum and dad went to eat in the family room of the pub down the road.

"Nice pub," said Shona's mum, as they studied the menu. "I wonder if the Old Bull used to look like this in the past?"

"Staying at the Old Bull Inn, are you?" asked the friendly landlord. He leaned

across the bar and winked at Shona.
"Has links with a famous highwayman,
that place, m'dear. Had you heard?"

Shona shook her head.

"How about that!" said Dad. "What
was his name?"

"His name was Captain Trevelyan."

Shona looked at the landlord sharply.

YOUNG HIPPO
READERS' CLUB
The sign of good storytelling!

A strange feeling had passed over her when he said that name.

"Did he have a horse?" she asked.

"Course he did. How could he be a highwayman, without a horse?"

Shona swallowed.

"What was his horse called?" she asked.

"His horse was as famous as he was," said the landlord. "Its name was Whistlejacket."

Shona's heart leapt with excitement. She pictured the magnificent ghostly stallion in the stable. Whistlejacket! A name to suit a horse like that, with a coat like polished steel. She pictured him galloping over the moor, as fast as the wind; as fast as a bullet fired from a pistol.

"Whistlejacket..." she murmured dreamily.

"There's a story about the two of them," said the landlord. "Want to hear it?"

Shona shivered with excitement. "Yes, please," she said.

"Well, one night, it's said that soldiers lay in wait for Captain Trevelyan at the Old Bull Inn. They planned to capture him and see him hanged.

"They heard the clip-clop of Whistlejacket's hooves down the dark, cobbled street and cocked their muskets.

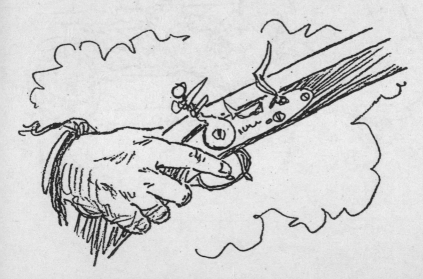

Then the horse came into view and – he was riderless!"

"Where was Captain Trevelyan?"

"Nobody knew. Had he been tipped off about the trap? Had he suffered an accident – or what?

"Anyway, they had the horse. They cornered it in the inn yard. They tied it into a stall with the stoutest rope they could find, and barred it in with the stoutest bars."

"Poor Whistlejacket!"

"Captain Trevelyan loved that horse. There was no way he'd be separated from it, alive or dead. So they waited for him to appear. They say the horse was there for days, and it would neither eat nor drink. But Captain Trevelyan never showed up. From time to time, though, a low whistle could be heard, like the master was calling him. And when the horse heard that whistle, he went mad! He crashed his hooves against the stall and fought like a fury to free himself. But they'd tied him up so tight, and barred him in so well, he couldn't get out.

"And then, one morning, they found he'd stopped his struggling. He'd given up and breathed his last."

"Ugh!" said Mum. "That's not a very nice tale! And then, I suppose, they captured Captain Trevelyan and hanged him?"

"Nobody knows what happened to Captain Trevelyan. They say he was never seen again."

"Hey, come on, Shona – eat up!" urged Dad. "I thought you were hungry."

"It's the landlord's fault," muttered Mum. "Filling her head with scary tales about highwaymen. She'll be having nightmares next."

"Don't worry about it, Shona," said her dad. "It's only an old story. They probably made it up for the tourists. I bet Captain Trevelyan never really existed."

"Whistlejacket did," said Shona softly to herself. "Poor Whistlejacket did."

Her lips trembled. She was trying not to cry.

Chapter 5

That night, Shona woke up suddenly. The bedroom was dark; it was just after midnight. Something had woken her. She listened hard. A sound came, faint but shrill. It sounded like a whistle.

And then she heard another noise. It was the whinny of a horse. Again the whistle came and again the whinny, answering it.

Then a crashing and a pounding started – fit to raise the dead!

"Whistlejacket!" Shona muttered and her heart went thump, thump, thump. "The ghost of Captain Trevelyan is whistling for him, like the landlord said, and he's trying to escape!"

In a panic, she climbed out of bed and headed for the safety of her parents' room.

They were fast asleep. Through all that
noise! She wondered whether to wake
them. No. Whistlejacket had faded away
at the sound of her mother's voice that
afternoon. He had chosen to appear only
to her. So perhaps she was the only one
who could hear him now?

Whistlejacket whinnied again. An
urgent call. A call that seemed to be for
her.

"He wants me to help him escape!"
gasped Shona. "That's what he wants!"

Shona shrank back against the landing wall. Her heart went out to the poor, trapped creature, but she was shaking with fear.

How could a girl who was afraid of horses help a magnificent, ghostly stallion in a frenzy to escape from his stall in the middle of the night?

And what about Captain Trevelyan? He had whistled, so his ghost must be out there somewhere, prowling around in the dark.

Again the stallion called to Shona. Again he pounded at his stall.

"Why have you chosen *me?*" she wailed.

She covered her ears, but the pleading call echoed inside her head. She knew she would never be able to forget that call. Or to forgive herself, if she let him down. If she did nothing at all to help. She *had* to conquer her fear.

One, two, *three*! She drew a deep breath and plunged towards the moonlit stairs, raced down and let herself out into the yard. The chilly night air struck through her pyjamas and the mossy cobblestones felt cold and damp beneath her feet.

She tried not to look at the shadows lurking on the edges of the yard as she ran across.

She creaked open the stable door. It was warm inside and reeked of horse. A dim light shone from an old-fashioned lantern, close to Whistlejacket's stall.

Shona saw him. He was rearing and tugging and straining at the rough rope halter; he was throwing and cutting himself against the sides of the stall and pounding at the planks of wood with his hooves. The air was full of flying strands of straw and dust.

Shona cowered back and stared. She felt so small and useless. But she felt full of pity, too.

Out of pity she murmured, "Calm down, Whistlejacket. Calm down. Please don't hurt yourself any more. Please!"

The stallion heard her voice and pricked his ears. His eyes still rolled wildly and his flanks heaved and shook. But his rearing and pounding stopped. He went very still, waiting. Waiting for her to draw near.

The scary smell of horse was overpowering. And though he was very still, Shona feared Whistlejacket's tremendous power, which she knew she couldn't control.

But he was injured and a prisoner. If only she could conquer her fear of him, Whistlejacket could be free.

Shona forced herself forward. She tugged and heaved at the stout bars across the stall until she managed to move them. That gave her confidence. Gathering up all her courage, she stepped into the stall.

Whistlejacket stood so still and calm, he scarcely seemed to breathe.

Shona eyed the halter and gasped in despair. The horse's straining, tossing head had tightened the simple knots in the stout, old rope. She feared her trembling hands could never undo them.

But at that moment, Whistlejacket gently lowered his head, lessening the strain on the rope. The knots slackened just enough for Shona's nimble fingers to work on them, tugging and pulling until, at last, she had done it – she had set him free!

Whistlejacket tossed and shook his head in excitement and delight – free at last of that dreadful rope. And Shona felt so full of relief and happiness for him, she wanted to clap and cheer.

Then gently, Whistlejacket bent and nuzzled her hand in gratitude. Shona timidly stroked his muzzle, and suddenly, in a rush of warmth, she put her arms around his neck and hugged him and realized that her fear had gone. Whistlejacket had helped her to conquer her fear. They had helped each other.

And then the whistle came again.

Whistlejacket pricked up his ears and snorted. Then he backed gently out of the stall. With a soft whinny of farewell, he trotted off into the dark, starry night to join his master.

Shona ran after him to the stable door. "Goodbye, Whistlejacket!" she cried.

Across the yard, Whistlejacket turned. Upon his back now gleamed an old-fashioned saddle. And in the saddle was a shadowy figure. A figure that waved a friendly arm to Shona, as though in thanks.

With a plunge of hooves, Whistlejacket and his rider leapt into the shadows and were gone. After more than two hundred years, the highwayman and his horse were together again.

Shona ran shivering back across the quiet yard. She didn't feel afraid of the shadows any more.

As she lay in bed, she pictured Whistlejacket with Captain Trevelyan on his back, galloping joyfully over the rolling moorland, his mane and tail flying in the wind. Free.

She felt happy for them. But, deep down, she couldn't help feeling sad for herself, and a little envious of Captain Trevelyan.

The ghost horse had conquered her fear and she had set him free. But now she would never be able to see or touch the beautiful creature again. She longed to see him, just one more time.

Chapter 6

Next day, Shona and her parents went to the seaside. Afterwards, they drove back across the moor. From time to time Shona caught glimpses of the wild ponies that lived there. And other horses with riders on their backs, hired out from local farms. Her eyes searched the rolling fields, the bleak, barren places and the deep green valleys, full of trees. But there was no sign of the one horse she wanted so much to see. If only she could see Whistlejacket, just one more time...

That night, Shona couldn't sleep. She felt all fizzed up inside, as though something exciting was about to happen. The hands on her travel alarm clock said nearly midnight. Still she hadn't slept a wink.

Suddenly she heard a sound.

She shot up in bed and listened hard.

Clip-clop, clip-clop, clip-clop.

Next minute she was at the window.
Bursting with joy, she was leaning out
beneath the thick, sweet-smelling
thatch.

Clip-clop, clip-clop, clip-clop.

Along the street trotted Whistlejacket,
fearless and proud, his head held high.
The old-fashioned saddle was on his
back. But this time it was empty. He had
come alone.

The stallion stopped beneath her window and looked up. He called softly to her and pawed the ground. And then he stood, very still, beside the big, stone mounting block. Waiting.

"Waiting for me!" gasped Shona. "He wants me to ride him!"

She pulled a sweater and a pair of jeans over her pyjamas and thrust her feet into a pair of trainers.

She let herself out of the old front door and ran across to the mounting block. She felt no fear as she clambered into the saddle and took a firm grasp of the pommel.

Then off Whistlejacket flew up the village street, as smooth and swift as a bird, with Shona on his back.

Out of the village and into the moonlit countryside they galloped. Over an ancient, hump-backed bridge. Along a valley, its steep sides wooded with fir and beech. Branches made a dark, mysterious tunnel over their heads. And beside the narrow path, a stream sparkled and splashed and tumbled.

Then the moor. Vast and rolling, mile after mile; silver-tinted under the bright full moon. Shona felt Whistlejacket's thrill as he leapt forward, flying over the highest part of the moor – on top of the world, it seemed.

This was *really* riding! Shona thought.
This was sensational!

Down to their right sparkled an inlet
of the sea.

No sooner had Shona seen it and wished, than they were there. Galloping along the beach with the spray in their faces and the wind in their hair. Shona laughed and shouted with pleasure. On the back of the beautiful Whistlejacket she felt no hint of fear.

Back through sleeping villages and lonely valleys they flew. Back over the highest places on the moor where the whole world seemed theirs. And back at last to their own village street and the mounting block by the Old Bull Inn.

Patiently Whistlejacket waited for Shona to dismount. She gave him one last hug, and then he turned away.

Sadly Shona wiped away a tear as Whistlejacket clip-clopped away from her, back up the village street towards the moor.

As he reached the very last house, there came a ghostly whistle, thin and shrill on the still night air. Then a figure sprang from the shadows and leapt up into the saddle. It was Captain Trevelyan. The dashing highwayman turned and doffed his hat to her. A last goodbye. Then Whistlejacket reared and plunged, his hooves sending up sparks from the cobblestones, and the beautiful ghost horse and his master were gone for good. Free at last to chase the wind across the moor, for ever and ever.

Chapter 7

Next morning, Shona awoke with a
heavy sadness in her heart. As though
she had awoken from a beautiful dream
she would never be able to recapture.

And then she remembered how
Whistlejacket and Captain Trevelyan
had shown their gratitude to her by
giving her that ride. Pleasure and sadness

72

were rolled into one as Shona relived the ride that was beyond anything this world could offer.

Shona got out of bed and pulled on her sweater and jeans which were in an untidy bundle on the floor. On the front of her sweater was a hair. It was a pure white hair, as smooth as a thread of silk.

A hair from Whistlejacket's mane!

Shona looked at the hair and her sadness faded. Something of Whistlejacket remained.

She took off the silver locket she wore around her neck. She twisted the hair into a little knot and locked it safe inside.

"Mum," said Shona at breakfast, "what are we doing today?"

"What would you like to do?" asked Shona's mum. "Shall we take a picnic on to the moors?"

"I'd like to go riding," said Shona.

"What? Riding? You've changed your mind? I don't believe it!"

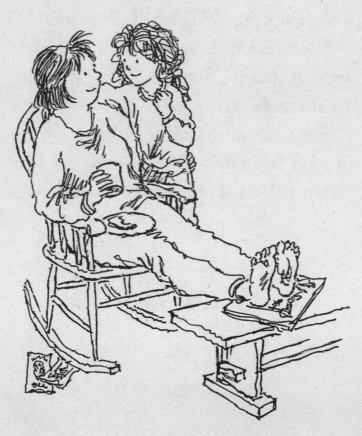

Shona's parents went riding with her. Her dad had a big bay horse called Drummond; her mum had a pretty mare called Janey. Shona herself had a small piebald pony called Aladdin.

Shona mounted Aladdin a little nervously, but with determination too.

The thrilling ride on Whistlejacket had made her determined to ride again.

Determined to become a really first-rate rider, like Captain Trevelyan.

They went for a long trek over the moor, discovering places they could never have reached on foot. It was a glorious day. The sun shone; the yellow flowers on the gorse bushes glowed; and

in the distance, the sea sparkled and
danced. Shona found she was having
a wonderful time. Aladdin was kind
and willing and obeyed her every move –
so small and controllable, after
Whistlejacket! With each minute that
passed, her confidence increased and her
enjoyment grew.

"Shona's riding has improved no end, hasn't it?" Dad marvelled. "All her confidence has returned. In fact – I think it's doubled!"

"Like magic! agreed Mum, proudly.

Shona smiled and touched the silver locket round her neck. No magic. It was Whistlejacket who had given her back her confidence, in return for his freedom. She would never forget that.

Shona knew she would always enjoy riding from now on. She would have some wonderful rides and know some beautiful horses.

But no ride would be as special as her night-time ride across the moor.

And no horse would ever be as beautiful as the ghost horse, Whistlejacket.

The End